NOAH'S ARK

Illustrated by MADA Design, Inc.
Adapted and written by David Bauman

© 2005 by Meredith Corporation, Des Moines, Iowa.
First edition. All Rights Reserved.
Printed in Mexico
ISBN: 0-696-22826-2

Meredith® Books
Des Moines, Iowa

Thousands of years ago, the earth was beautiful. The weather was perfect and there was no rain, thunder, or lightning. Animals, from lions and monkeys to the smallest mouse and the biggest elephant, roamed freely. The sky was filled with dragonflies and doves. The water was filled with fish and ducks.

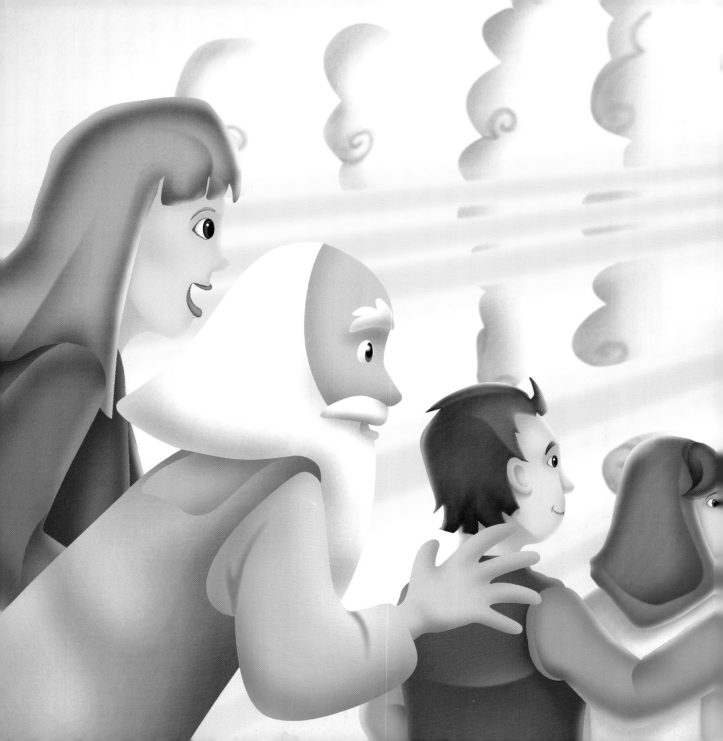

At this time lived Noah, a man who loved God. He, his wife, and their three sons and their wives raised sheep and grew crops. The family sang joyful songs to God and played music for Him.

But God was unhappy because other people did not obey Him. God told Noah that a great flood would soon cover the earth and that Noah should build a big boat, or Ark, for his family and all the animals to live in during the flood.

Noah and his sons built the Ark according to God's plans. The family made a giant door on the side where people and animals could enter. Meanwhile, Noah's wife and their sons' wives gathered the food they would need.

People laughed when they saw what Noah was doing. They didn't believe what God had told Noah about the flood.

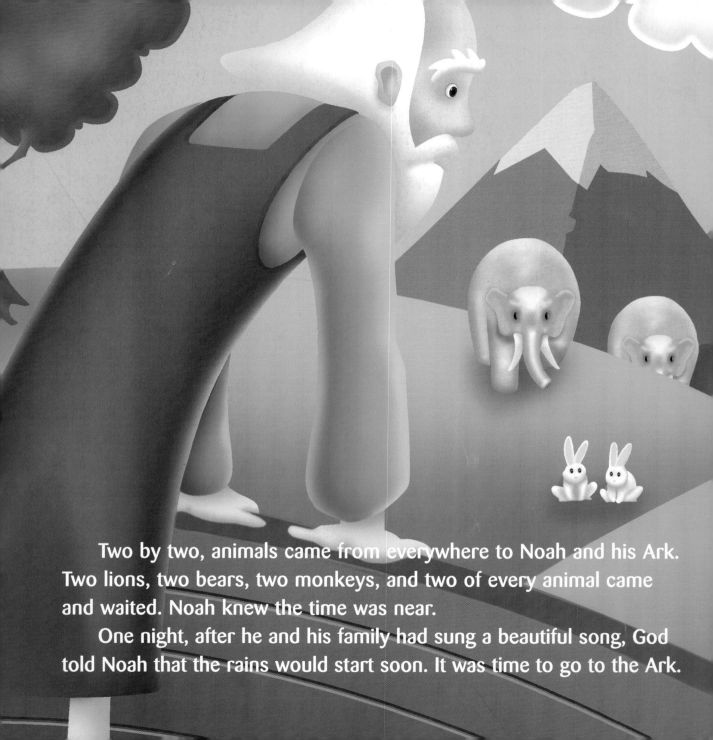

Two by two, animals came from everywhere to Noah and his Ark. Two lions, two bears, two monkeys, and two of every animal came and waited. Noah knew the time was near.

One night, after he and his family had sung a beautiful song, God told Noah that the rains would start soon. It was time to go to the Ark.

The next day, Noah opened the giant door. He and his family climbed in.

Birds, animals, and all living things followed Noah into the Ark. People laughed at Noah and his Ark.

God shut the door and the rains began. Noah and his family prayed. It rained for 40 days and 40 nights. The Ark rubbed the rocks as the water lifted it higher and higher. Thunder and lightning shook the Ark.

Finally it stopped raining. God heard the sheep, the monkeys, the ducks, and all the other animals. The music and prayers from Noah's family reminded God of his promise to Noah.

God made the floodwaters go away. Noah and his family could feel the bottom of the Ark rubbing a mountaintop.

Noah sent out a raven to look for land. It flew and flew.
Next he sent out a dove, but it came back. A few days later, Noah
sent out another dove, and it returned with an olive branch in its mouth.
Noah's family now knew there was enough dry land for trees to grow!

Seven days later the dove was sent out again, and it didn't return. Noah knew this meant the dove could land, and it was time to leave the Ark.

Noah opened the giant door, and the lions and elephants, monkeys and sheep, and all the birds and living things left the Ark, two by two.

Noah built an altar to honor God. The animals watched as Noah and his family sang a joyful song to Him.

God blessed Noah and his family for being faithful to Him, and God promised to never flood the Earth again.